SAMMY
AND THE
STARMAN

ANNE CASSIDY
Illustrated by Tony Ross

Barrington Stoke

First published in 2006 in Great Britain by
Barrington Stoke Ltd
18 Walker Street, Edinburgh, EH3 7LP

www.barringtonstoke.co.uk

This edition first published 2013

ISBN: 978-1-78112-219-8

Printed in China by Leo

Contents

Chapter 1
Post 342

When Sammy Parker saw the rocket lying on the grass he knew right away that it was from another planet.

Sammy was in Jupiter Park. He was walking along when he saw the rocket sticking up out of the long grass. He stood still for a moment. He was startled. What had he found? Sammy looked up at the sky in case there was a spaceship there looking as if it had lost something. But there was only the sun, shining at him from the corner of an empty blue sky. It looked very quiet up there, like the road outside on Christmas Day, when everyone is indoors eating turkey.

Sammy bent down and looked closely at the rocket. It was the shape of a fat drain pipe. Some parts of it were black and sooty. It looked a bit worn out as if it had travelled a long way. It was made of an odd silver metal with lines running down it.

When he was sure the rocket wasn't going to shoot off back into the sky, Sammy put out his hand and touched each end of it. It was about half a metre long. Sammy put his hands carefully under the rocket and picked it up. It was light, he could hardly feel he was carrying it. As he stood there, holding the rocket, Sammy felt a kind of warm glow coming from it. It was rather like picking up the electric kettle after his dad had made a mug of tea. Sammy made up his mind to take the rocket home so that he could look at it more closely.

Just then he heard the sound of someone wheezing and panting. He knew who it was. Dennis Frogman, the boy from next door.

"What you doing?" Dennis said in a loud voice.

Dennis had red hair which stuck up as if he'd just seen a ghost. He always seemed to have his mouth open and sometimes there was an inhaler sticking out of it.

He was not Sammy's favourite person.

"I found this," Sammy said. "It looks like an engine of some sort."

He didn't say *rocket* on purpose. He knew that Dennis would make fun of him.

"Let me see," Dennis said, and he grabbed the rocket out of Sammy's hands.

Sammy took off his glasses and cleaned them on his T-shirt. Dennis never asked for things. He just took what he wanted. The other kids in class let him. Dennis liked fights and he was good at punching people.

Dennis looked at the rocket for a few moments. Sammy could tell he wasn't sure about what it was. He held it up to the sun and screwed his eyes up so as to see it better. Then, without warning, Dennis tossed the rocket into the air.

"No!" Sammy shouted.

The rocket bounced onto the grass.

"It's just a load of old rubbish," Dennis said and walked away.

Sammy rushed over and picked up the rocket. He felt it all over. There didn't seem to be any damage. He looked round. Dennis was at the other end of the park. He was looking at a pile of old cardboard boxes that had been dumped.

Sammy decided to go home. He picked up the rocket and held it gently in his arms. He left the park and walked carefully along the street. He felt as if he were carrying something very important, like his gran's china teapot.

When he was near home he looked down at the metal on the rocket and saw some letters and numbers on it. He stopped and turned the rocket round until the sun shone on the letters and he could read them properly – POST 342.

It was the first thing he had found out about this rocket ship. Its name was POST 342.

Chapter 2
The Letters to Plar

As soon as he got home, Sammy went to his workshop at the bottom of the back garden. He edged his way carefully past the shed door so that he didn't scrape the sides of the rocket or knock it into the lawn mower. He laid it on a long bench and rested for a moment.

He got some paper out and started to jot down some notes. He made a quick diagram to show the shape of the rocket and the type of metal covering. He wrote the date and the time and where he'd found it. He measured the rocket with his wind-up metal measuring tape. He'd been right. It was about half a metre long – 56 centimetres to be exact.

Sammy stepped back to look at the rocket. A feeling of delight purred away in his stomach. He got his magnifying glass out of his pocket and inspected the metal again. He was looking at the very tip of the rocket when a noise from outside made him stop. He tutted and looked out of the shed door. It sounded like Dennis Frogman in his garden next door.

Sammy walked towards the fence and looked through his spy hole. He didn't make a sound. Dennis was inside his treehouse. He was standing on the small wooden deck, his hand up over his eyes as if he was the captain of a ship. Sammy looked at his big face under the mop of red hair. He let his eyes go into a blur and tried to read the boy's mind. As he tried to see inside Dennis's head, Sammy began to feel dizzy but he snapped awake when Dennis jumped off the treehouse and ran inside.

Sammy looked at the treehouse which Mr Frogman had built for Dennis. It was on two levels. There was a wooden deck, then a small ladder led up three rungs into a small house. Sammy loved that treehouse. He knew that Dennis and some of his school friends had taken their sleeping bags and slept there a couple of times. He'd seen their torches from his bedroom window.

Dennis had never asked him to play in the treehouse. Sammy took his glasses off and gave a long sigh. He cleaned them with the end of his T-shirt. It was lucky that he had more important things to worry about. His rocket.

He went back to the shed and began to polish it with some old rags. He took great care to wipe around the letters that said POST 342. When he turned the rocket over to clean the other side he heard a rattling sound. Right away he was worried. He remembered how Dennis had thrown it into the air. Something inside the rocket may have broken. Sammy turned it upside down gently and gave it a little shake.

Nothing happened for a moment and then a few tiny bits of paper floated out and spread across the worktop. Sammy stepped back in surprise. Then he bent down until his nose was almost touching them. At first he thought he was seeing things. He rubbed at the corners of his eyes and with his fingers he pulled apart the tiny bits of paper that had fallen out.

It couldn't be.

There were about 20 bits of paper in all. Tiny rectangles, all white, with small markings on them. Each of them had a tiny coloured sticker in the corner. Sammy couldn't believe his eyes.

He picked up the magnifying glass. He thought he knew what these bits of paper were but he wanted to look at them close up. He looked through the lens at the tiny markings. It was print, in one line, from one side to the other.

Jix Langer 4th, 62, Condo, Sector 8, East Plar

He picked up another one and looked again.

Serry Pop 2nd, 1579 Sees Edge, Sector 24, East Plar

He put all the bits of paper in a line on the table in front of him. There were 21 of them. Each was one centimetre long.

They were tiny letters with stamps on.

Chapter 3
The Starman

Sammy had always known that there was something important up in the sky. When he was very little he had thought that the stars were lights from Other Worlds. Planets like Earth. Full of people and buildings and cars. But as he got older he understood a lot more about the sky.

His dad found an old telescope at a car boot sale. Sammy helped him to repair it, to oil it and polish its parts. They set it up in the loft,

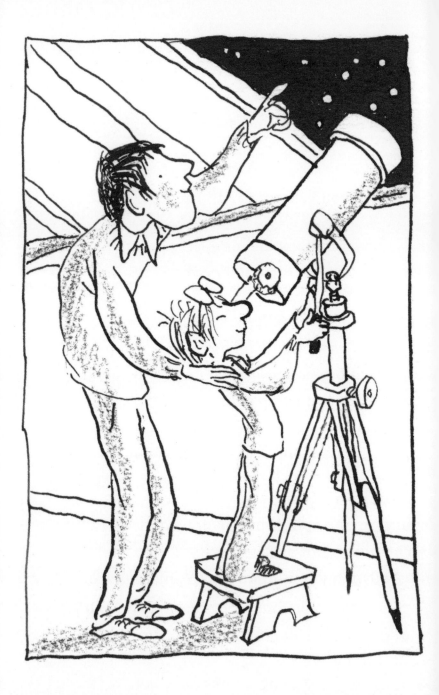

next to the skylight, so that they could look deep into the sky. Sammy loved that telescope. He measured it and drew a diagram of it. He cleaned and dusted it, taking extra care of the lens caps.

Sammy's dad explained that stars were not lights from other worlds. Stars were really big bundles of burning gas that sat in the middle of nowhere. Like the sun that Sammy looked up at every day. But the sun was close by and stars were much further away. Like London was just a train ride away from where they lived but Australia was a very long plane journey.

The sky turned out to be a very big place. And it wasn't a flat thing, as Sammy had thought, but the beginning of Space. This was an everlasting place that was deeper than the deepest hole in the ground and wider even than all the oceans put together and stretched out. It was so big that nobody could measure it properly. It was called the Universe and nobody knew for sure how it had all started or what happened there.

Sammy's dad put a stool in front of his telescope so that Sammy could look through and see the stars. On a clear night he could see all the different patterns and groups of stars – the constellations.

"Are there many stars and planets?"

"Too many to count," his dad replied.

"Does anyone live on them?" Sammy asked.

His dad had given a shrug as if to say, 'Maybe. Maybe not.'

There were stories of Flying Saucers and men from Mars. He'd seen pictures of creatures with egg heads and saucer eyes. They were grey and had skinny legs and arms. Some people called them aliens but Sammy didn't like this word. It sounded unfriendly. It was as if these creatures arrived on Earth intending to quarrel with humans the moment they set eyes on them.

Sammy had looked in wonder at the night sky. All those stars, all those planets. How could all those places be empty? It didn't make sense. There had to be Other Worlds, Other Living Creatures.

Now he had found some real proof. He had a rocket with the letters POST 342 on its side. He also had 21 tiny letters.

All he had to do was to find out where they had come from.

After tea he asked if he could go back to Jupiter Park because he'd lost something. He took a rucksack with him. In it he put his measuring tape, a magnifying glass and a torch, as well as some pencils and paper. Who knew what he'd find there?

The first thing that caught his eye was the pile of boxes, sitting on the ground. He walked over to the pile and took out his magnifying glass and looked at it. He could see huge ants walking in a line across it and a giant slug moving across it the other way. Sammy began to worry that they might crash when he heard a strange sound. A nose-blowing sound. He looked around. The only person he could see was in the street outside the park and he wasn't blowing his nose.

Then Sammy looked down under the boxes. He heard it again. Someone blowing their nose. A tiny hooting sound but Sammy could hear it very clearly. He knelt down and held his breath. There was a gap between two of the boxes like a cave. Sammy bent down but still he could only see darkness. As he opened his rucksack and got his torch out he heard another sound.

"Nix, Nix, Nix!"

A voice, thin and croaky. He shone a light into the space under the boxes. There, looking very cross, was a small man. A very small man.

"Get that light out of my eyes," he said, in a grumpy voice.

Sammy clicked the torch off and looked into the dark again. At first he couldn't see anything much and then, suddenly, just in front of his feet, he saw a small, angry face.

"You took your time. I mean, toxic tigers, I could have been here for a good ten years and you might not have sighted me!"

"Sorry," Sammy said, looking up and down at the small man.

"But you sighted the rocketzoom."

He meant the rocket ship, Sammy was sure.

"I took it back to my workshop," he said.

"First rate, Earth Boy. Take me to it! I'm stellar years behind my deadlines. Hurry up. Hurry up!"

Sammy put his hand into the dark space and the tiny man stepped onto it. He was about 15 centimetres tall and much more heavy than Sammy had expected.

"Put me somewhere secret, Earth Boy. I don't want to be sighted!"

Sammy unzipped his rucksack and put the Starman gently down into it. He could still hear his voice, babbling away.

"Nix Pix! If I'm late again with the post I'll be tweezered good and proper."

"Tweezered?" Sammy whispered into his rucksack, "What's that?"

"You don't want to know, Earth Boy. Can't you speed up a bit? I haven't got 999 years to sit on my bum!"

Sammy zipped his rucksack shut. He could feel the little man inside. He looked around to make sure there was no one watching him, then he walked quickly back home.

Chapter 4
Jax

Sammy took the Starman out of his rucksack and put him on the worktop in the shed, next to his rocket. The Starman looked at the tiny white envelopes and clapped his hands.

"The post! The post! Thank Crozzers you found it!"

The Starman sat cross-legged and started to sort the letters. He mumbled all the time as he was doing it. Now Sammy had a chance to have a really good look at him.

He was wearing a white space suit. Across his back were the letters POST. And in smaller writing the number 342. He looked fit. His body was solid and his legs and arms were strong. His face and hair were odd though. He had lots of wrinkles on his face as if he was old and his hair was white and hung in a pigtail right down his back.

The Starman stood up and left the letters in piles. He walked round the rocket looking closely at it. Then he stood back with his hands on his hips. He looked fed-up and a bit puzzled.

"My name's Sammy Parker," Sammy said. He thought it was time they got to know each other better. "What's yours?"

"Jax Bord 3rd," said the Starman, looking round. "You can call me Jax."

"Where do you come from?" Sammy said. The name *Jax* sounded very odd to him.

"Plar, of course!"

Jax's voice was annoyed as if Sammy should have known that already.

"Is that a planet?"

"A very small planet. It's divided into North, South, East and West. I, myself, live in South

Plar where it's warm and we sight a lot of sunrays."

"Oh," Sammy said. "Have you lived there long?"

"Yex, all my life so far. 397 years."

Sammy was amazed. Jax leaned on Sammy's torch and explained.

"Because we're smaller we live a lot longer than you Earth People. That's why we're more advanced than you. I'm not that old. My father, Jax Bord 2nd, now he's getting on – 526."

"That's really old!" Sammy said.

"We have time to develop our brains. That's why we invented things a long time before you. Train lines. The moto drive. Tricity. Rocketzoom. You name it and we invented it first."

Jax was looking very pleased with himself.

"But we invented those things too," Sammy said. He had read all about how the railways and the motor car had been invented.

"Nix," Jax said and shook his head so that his pigtail moved from one side to the other. "We invented them and then we left some important clues for your scientists."

"Really?" Sammy said.

"You found some things out on your own but we had to give you a bit of help."

"Cool," Sammy said.

Jax went up to the rocket again. He put his hand out to touch one of the grooves and a door opened suddenly. He picked up his letters and took them into the rocket. Sammy was left on his own and felt a bit lonely. But then he heard lots of sounds from inside the rocket, doors opening and shutting and things being moved about. He could also hear a lot of angry words.

"Blistering boils, what's happened here! I'll never get this post through. I'll be tweezered!"

Jax's head popped out of the rocket again. His tiny face was looking flushed and there was a smear of what looked like oil on his forehead.

"The rocket's gubbered. I'll need to get in touch with Rocket Rescue. They'll come and pick me up."

"Gubbered?" Sammy said. What could be wrong with it?

"Yex. It's the rotix. It's come away from the gazgox so the gaz won't flow. It must have cracked when we landed."

Sammy nodded, even though he had no idea what Jax was talking about.

"These letters. They're due at East Plar at 80 minutes past the midday chime. If I don't get them there I'll be tweezered!"

"What is *tweezered?*" Sammy asked. He didn't like the sound of it at all.

"You're too young to find out about such things," Jax said and rubbed his tiny hands together. "I'm in trouble. Landing on Earth is not allowed without a Visitor's Permit 1592X. It's strictly forbidden. I've got letters and box-wraps in here which I must deliver! NOW!"

And then a very odd thing happened.

Jax lay down and closed his eyes. Within seconds he seemed to sink into a deep sleep.

"Jax?" Sammy whispered.

But the Starman didn't answer and didn't move. Sammy felt scared for a moment. Was Jax all right? Had he passed out? Was he ill?

He got his magnifying glass and held it over the Starman. He looked carefully at him. The tiny man was very still but he could just see his chest rising and falling. He was just about to look for a cloth to put over him when the shed door banged open and the sound of wheezing and panting came from behind.

Dennis Frogman stood there.

"What do you want?" Sammy said.

Dennis was looking all over the worktop to see what Sammy had there.

"What's that?" he said, "That metal thing, on the worktop?"

Sammy didn't know what to do. He tried to act normally.

"It's a rocket."

"Not that! The other thing, on the table."

Dennis leaned across and pointed at Jax.

Sammy thought fast. "It's a figure from Star Wars that I found at a car boot sale," he said.

Dennis didn't say anything for a moment and then put his finger out as if to touch.

"You can't touch it," Sammy said quickly. "It's still wet. I had to glue it back together."

"Star Wars?" Dennis said. "I don't remember any figure like that in Star Wars!"

Sammy didn't answer. He took his glasses off and cleaned them with his T-shirt. He held his breath until Dennis turned away. Just then the Starman moved a little and made a sound.

"What was that?" said Dennis, turning back.

Sammy coughed.

"I've got a cold," he said.

Dennis looked at him. Sammy could tell he didn't believe him. Then Dennis took his blue inhaler out of his pocket and put it into his mouth. Without another word he went out into the garden. Sammy closed the shed door quickly and locked it. He stood very still. He could feel his heart thumping hard. Jax was waking up and stretched his arms above his head. Then, just as quickly as he'd gone off to sleep, the small man was standing up looking fresh and full of energy. In his hand he held something that looked like a tiny mobile phone.

"This is my stellar beacon. If I point this in the direction of Plar and turn it on, Rocket Rescue will come and collect me. But I need to be somewhere high."

"I know," Sammy said, "we'll go up to the loft."

He put the Starman in his pocket and looked out of the shed door before running across the garden and into the house.

Chapter 5
The Planet Plar

Jax stood under the skylight and held up his stellar beacon. He pointed it at the sky. Sammy expected to see a beam of light but there was nothing. When the tiny man had finished he turned back and looked at Sammy's telescope.

"Dusty daggers," he said to Sammy. "That is basic. I thought Earth people were more advanced."

Jax climbed up onto the stool by the telescope. He stood on tiptoes to look through the lens. Sammy pulled down the telescope so Jax could reach it to look at the sky.

"I can't even sight Plar," Jax said.

"How far away is it?" Sammy asked.

"On the other side of the moon. We're close but tiny. That's why Earth people can't sight us with their most powerful lens. They think that we're just some rubbish flying about in Space."

"Oh!"

"It's for the best. If Earth people discovered Plar they'd be trampling all over us in no time. That's why I've got to get the rocketzoom back. Leaving a postship on Earth. It's the worst crime in the Plar. Once Earth people find out about us, we're tweezered."

It was true. Earth people might go to Plar and squash buildings or even whole towns. Sammy thought of an Earth rocket landing on Plar. A great shadow would fall across the tiny houses and cars. He saw it land with a thump in the middle of some nice street in South Plar where Jax lived. Then someone like Dennis Frogman would get out. Sammy thought all the residents would look up into the sky at this giant boy. Would they all look a bit like Jax? Strong but old, their bodies firm but their faces lined with age? They would look up at horrible Dennis. He would most likely shout at them. His voice might split their eardrums.

Outside it was getting dark and a bit cold. Sammy picked up his jacket and put Jax in the inside pocket. They went downstairs. There were lights in the next garden and Sammy thought he could hear Dennis's voice down by the treehouse. He walked towards the shed. Everything was working out fine. It wouldn't be long before Jax and his letters and his post ship were on their way back to Plar.

When he opened the shed door the workshop looked odd. He clicked the light switch on and looked around. Everything was in its place but there was something different about it. Then he noticed a big empty space on the worktop. He gasped.

"What's the matter, Sammy?"

Jax's voice came from down in his pocket.

"The rocket's gone!"

"Nix Pix!" said Jax. He struggled to get out and climbed onto the worktop. "Now I'll never get back to Plar!"

Sammy walked quickly out into the garden and over to the spy hole. Jax had climbed up on to his shoulder. Through the hole in the fence he could see Dennis sitting cross-legged on the

wooden deck of the treehouse. He was holding something. Then he turned round and Sammy saw he had the rocket.

"Have you sighted it?" Jax said, his mouth close to Sammy's ear.

"Dennis Frogman stole it!" Sammy said, in an angry hiss.

"Show me," Jax said.

Sammy held the Starman up to the spy hole. He felt the small man's body tense and then watched him make his hands into fists.

"Poisonous panthers," he said. "Now what am I going to do? I must have that rocketzoom back. If I don't I may never be able to go home."

"I'll have to go in there and get it," Sammy said, but he felt rather nervous.

"Demand it back!" hissed Jax. "Say you'll gubber him!"

Just then there was a shout from the house next door. It sounded like Dennis's mum. Dennis stopped what he was doing. He looked annoyed. He climbed down from the deck of his treehouse. Then he ran up the garden to his house.

"He's gone!" Sammy said. "I could get over the fence and take it back."

"Right from under his nasty nose," Jax said, his tiny arms flying around with excitement.

Sammy put Jax back in his pocket and got a red plastic box from the shed. He placed it upside down by the spy hole and climbed over the fence.

It was very dark.

He stopped for a moment, hidden from view by bushes. There were sounds coming from every direction. A bird hooted. A cat hissed. A dog barked angrily a couple of gardens away. He felt something brush past his leg and froze. A small creature shot off across the lawn.

He was scared. The treehouse seemed miles away.

He waited a few moments then he took four giant steps and ran the rest of the way to the treehouse. He jumped the three steps up onto the deck. His heart was beating fast.

"You all right, Sammy?" Jax whispered. His head was poking out of the pocket.

"We're here!" Sammy hissed back.

Even though it was dark Sammy could see the rocket on the deck. He bent down to see if it was all right. It was. Sammy felt like fainting with relief. Now all he had to do was take it back to the shed. Then Jax could wait for the Rocket Rescue and be on his way.

He took a quick look round the dark garden. His eyes flicked up to the first floor window where he knew Dennis's bedroom was. There was no light on. Most probably Dennis was watching the telly. He picked up the rocket and held it carefully.

"Everything's OK," he whispered down to Jax.

Then he stepped down from the treehouse.

The garden lights came on making Sammy jump with surprise. The lights were so bright, they dazzled him. In his ears he could hear a loud booming voice.

"Got yer!"

Dennis had been waiting for him to come.

Chapter 6
The Star Wars Figure

"That model rocket is mine," Dennis Frogman said. His face filled up all the space in front of Sammy's eyes. He grabbed the rocket out of Sammy's arms and dumped it back on the treehouse deck.

"I found it!" Sammy said. He pushed his hand into his jacket pocket to make sure Jax was quiet so Dennis wouldn't see him.

"You found it in Jupiter Park. So it wasn't yours to start with!" Dennis said.

"*You* said it was rubbish," Sammy hissed back. "You chucked it away. It could have broken."

The two boys stood face to face. Sammy hoped that Dennis wasn't going to use his fists. The rocket sat on the treehouse deck. Even in the dark you could see the words POST 342 on its side.

In his pocket Sammy could feel Jax moving around. The little man's shoulders were like steel and he was pushing himself about as though he was shadow boxing. The Starman was mad. Time was moving on. Sammy began to panic. He had to get the rocket back to his garden in time for Rocket Rescue.

"I'll swop you for it," Sammy said, suddenly.

"HA!" Dennis said. "What have you got that I'd want?"

Sammy felt Jax curl up in his pocket. His muscles and joints were still hard but he was like a ball.

"My telescope!" he said, and his heart sank.

Dennis looked surprised. Sammy had talked about his telescope at school. He'd said it was the most precious thing in his house.

"You can have it," Sammy repeated. "It's worth a lot more than this."

Dennis looked as if he was thinking hard. His red hair was sticking up more than usual. It was like an arrow pointing at the sky.

"Well?" Sammy said.

"Nope," Dennis suddenly said, "I don't want that load of old junk. I want your Star Wars figure. Then you can have this model rocket back."

Sammy stood very still. His Star Wars figure! He took his glasses off and cleaned them while he thought about it. It could work. It might work! He could feel Jax in his pocket. Had he heard what Dennis said? Would he think it was a good idea?

"All right," Sammy said, "I'll just get him ... I mean I'll just get it. You bring the rocket over to the fence and I'll get the figure. We'll swop."

Dennis nodded and Sammy sprinted over to the fence and got back into his own garden. He scooped Jax out of his pocket. He lifted him right up to his mouth and gave the lowest whisper he could, "You need to lie very still. Don't move at all. When Dennis isn't looking, you have to creep away. I'll wait here for you."

Jax nodded. He lay down on the red plastic box and seemed to go into a deep sleep. Dennis's head popped up over the fence.

"Here you are."

Dennis was holding the rocket in his arms as though it was a tray. Sammy took it and put it on the grass. Then he picked up the Starman and held him out to Dennis.

"I had to fix another bit of him ... it ... so the glue is still wet. He should just lie in one place till the morning. Then you'll be able to play with him."

"It's warm!" Dennis said.

"That's because he ... it's ... been in my pocket."

"Which Star Wars film was he in?" Dennis said.

"All of them," Sammy replied.

But Dennis wasn't there any more. He'd run off towards his treehouse. Sammy could see him jump up onto the deck and put something down on the wood. Sammy frowned. He took his glasses off and cleaned them with the end of his shirt.

Poor Jax. Would he be all right?

Chapter 7
Rocket Rescue

Sammy put the rocket in the middle of the lawn. He put it pointing up and it didn't fall over. It was pointing at the sky and it no longer looked like a bit of pipe but a spaceship in which Jax would get back to Plar.

Then he sat down, by the spy hole, and waited for Jax. He just hoped that the Starman would stay quite still for as long as it took for Dennis to get fed up.

What time would Rocket Rescue arrive? What would it look like? Sammy thought it might be a kind of helicopter with a steel tow rope which Jax would tie onto his craft. Would the rescue ship have flashing lights like the road rescue trucks he and his dad had sometimes used? They cost money, Sammy knew. Maybe Jax would have to pay to get his rocketzoom towed back to Plar.

After about ten minutes, Sammy began to feel a bit bored.

He looked carefully through the spy hole and saw that Dennis was still in the treehouse. It made him feel bad. He had left Jax there with Dennis. It had seemed like a good idea at the time but a feeling of worry was wriggling around inside him like a tiny worm. He could see Dennis moving around. For all he knew Dennis was playing games with Jax, moving his arms and legs. The thought of it made him shiver.

Sammy was starting to feel trapped himself. His legs wanted to get up and go back over the fence to rescue Jax. But that was no good. Rocket Rescue would be along soon and he didn't want to risk Dennis seeing it.

He had to stay calm and just wait. Dennis would get bored and play with something else. Then Jax would creep out. Sammy just had to keep his eyes open and his mind alert so that he saw Jax when he escaped from the treehouse. He put his hand over his stomach to calm himself. Then he let his head rest back against the fence and gazed up at the sky.

The moon was a bright white colour, like an electric bulb that had been switched on. Around it the sky was deep navy blue and everywhere he looked were tiny stars. When he stared at them for a long time they seemed to flicker like the lights on a Christmas tree. Somewhere up there was Plar – North, South, East and West. He tried to picture it. A very small planet on which there lived a race of tiny people. Or maybe they were the right size and it was just that the people on Earth were giants. Then he thought of something weird. What if there was a much bigger planet, on the other side of the universe, where the creatures were huge and they made Earth people look tiny?

He sat up at the thought. And what if there was another planet, further away, that was bigger again?

This idea seemed to multiply inside his head until he couldn't think of another thing. He felt like his head was about to pop open until he heard a sound that startled him. He looked round the garden in a panic. Where was he? What was he supposed to be doing?

"Sammy! Are you there? I can't sight you anywhere!"

Looking round, in surprise, he saw Jax's face at the spy hole. It looked red and puffed out and

Sammy realized that the Starman must have climbed up. He stood up and picked Jax up from the fence and lifted him across to his garden.

He was puzzled. The lights in the treehouse were still on. How had Jax got away?

"Septic socks! That Earth Boy is very odd," Jax explained. "He went up to his home to get a drink. Then he was going to come back and change my clothes! I'd have been gubbered if I'd stayed."

"Oh!"

"Where's the rocketzoom?" Jax said.

"There!" Sammy said. He clicked on his torch and pointed it at the rocket.

Jax got his stellar beacon out and jabbed at it with his finger. He spoke softly into it as he walked towards the rocket. Sammy got up and followed him.

"Yex, they're almost here. I'll get inside and then they'll pick me up in a few Earth minutes. Sammy, I'm very grateful. You've been a good friend and I won't forget it."

Jax pulled open the door of the rocket and got in. Sammy heard a lot of noise from over the fence. A shout. A squeal. The sound of angry words coming closer. Dennis Frogman.

"Goodbye, Sammy Parker," Jax said and got into the rocket and closed the door behind him.

"You nicked my Star Wars figure!" Dennis shouted. He was climbing over the fence.

Sammy didn't answer. In the middle of the lawn, was the rocket. Inside it, waiting for the rescue ship, was Jax.

"I want it back," Dennis said, running up over the grass and grabbing Sammy. He pulled Sammy's elbow up behind his back.

Sammy felt pain shoot through his arm and he struggled. If only he could just stop Dennis from going over to the rocket!

"Where is it?" Dennis demanded.

"I don't know," Sammy said. He was wriggling hard so as to get free.

And that's when it happened.

The Rocket Rescue craft skimmed across the garden like an enormous Frisbee. It shot across the grass and up the far end, near the house. It looked like a glowing white light in the shape of a saucer. It stopped suddenly and hovered in the air and then swooped back down the garden towards them.

"What's that?" Dennis said.

It floated past Sammy's shoulder and then back in the other direction.

"Who threw that?" Dennis said. "It could have hit me!"

The white saucer did a U-turn and seemed to hang in the air for a moment. Sammy looked with wonder. All around it the air sparkled and fizzed as though millions of tiny bubbles were coming out. He rubbed his eyes as the craft seemed to glide towards the rocket and stop for a moment. Then it started to move back and forth as if it was parking in a small space. Finally, it began to move down to where the rocket stood.

"How did you make it do that?" Dennis said.

The spacecraft dropped down slowly until it was only centimetres from the top of the rocket.

"It must be powered by a remote!" Dennis said in a hushed voice.

A low and powerful sound came from the spacecraft. A buzzing noise, like the drill at the dentist's. Sammy held his breath wondering what was going to happen. The Rocket Rescue ship was shimmering in the night air. It shone out like a powerful neon light and Sammy was amazed that nobody was looking out of their windows to see what was happening.

The buzzing stopped suddenly and two doors fell open underneath the craft. Something was let down out of the craft but it was too small and too low for Sammy to see. Dennis took a step towards it but a bright blue light flashed in his direction and he stumbled back and fell onto the grass on his bottom.

Then the rocket began to rise as if it was being pulled into the craft. It went up slowly, carefully. Sammy took a step nearer and saw that the rocket was turning on its side. For a moment it looked as if it was part of the ship.

Then there was complete stillness. The Rocket Rescue ship just sat floating in the air like a feather on the wind. Sammy wanted to wave his hand and say goodbye to Jax but he kept his arms by his sides.

"Grab it!" Dennis whispered.

It started to move slowly up into the air until Sammy heard the noise of some sort of engine. It got louder and then the spaceship soared away in the night, above the trees and over the roof until it had completely vanished. Sammy watched it until the very last minute. When it was gone he felt suddenly worried and sad, as if he'd just lost something.

"What was all that?" Dennis said.

Sammy couldn't keep it a secret any more. He told the truth.

"That figure I gave you was a Starman from the Planet Plar. It's near the moon but nobody knows it's there because it's so small. His rocket crashed and he had to get a breakdown rocket to come and pick him up. That was what the flying saucer was. The Starman had to get back because he didn't have a visitor's permit. If any person from Plar leaves a rocket on Earth they get tweezered."

Dennis Frogman looked at Sammy as if he was mad.

"HA!" Dennis said.

"It's true!" Sammy said.

"Your dad bought it at a car boot sale."

Dennis walked off towards the fence and his own garden.

Chapter 8
A Letter from Space

Sammy tiptoed through the house and up the stairs to the loft. He opened the skylight. His arms and legs felt tired and slow but inside his head it was a different story. His brain was like a racing track, one thought speeding along after another. In his head he saw the rocketzoom being towed back to Plar. There were pictures of the rescue ship gliding round his garden, looking for the broken rocket. Dennis was there as well, a look of surprise and fright on his face. But the thing Sammy thought about most was the Starman, safe in his rocket, on his way home.

Sammy would miss Jax. He only hoped that the little man's ship wasn't totally gubbered.

He fixed up the telescope and looked at the night sky. There was a giant world out there that he wanted to know more about. He turned the telescope from one side to the other and the universe seemed to rush by him. He pointed the telescope at the moon and wondered which bit of it was closest to Plar.

He would never know because Plar was too small and anyway Earth scientists thought that it was a bit of floating Space rubbish. It would always be a secret, which was maybe for the best. Then Jax and his dad and everyone else on Plar could live quietly without Earth people bothering them.

His thoughts began to slow down until he was left with a picture of Jax, stopping his rocketzoom to deliver letters. Then he fell asleep.

Sammy's dad woke him the next morning.

"I've been looking all over for you, son. You've been up here all night!"

Sammy rubbed his eyes. His dad was holding a mug of tea.

"Sorry, I forgot all about going to bed," he said. He stood up and stretched his arms and legs.

"You missed all the excitement from last night. Some people in the street swear that they saw a flying saucer in the gardens. Honestly!" Sammy's dad said, putting the mug of tea down beside Sammy.

"Really?" Sammy said.

The door closed behind his dad and Sammy walked across to the skylight and reached up to shut it. Something on the floor caught his eye. A small white square of paper. He picked it up and held it between his finger and thumb. There were tiny letters on it and what looked like a tiny stamp in the corner. He pulled his magnifying glass out of his pocket and looked at it.

Sammy Parker, The Telescope Room, Earth

Suddenly he felt much better as if someone had just switched a light on inside him. He found a safety pin and opened the envelope with the sharp end. He unfolded the paper and read it out loud.

Dear Sammy,

I could not have got back to Plar without you. I'll never forget how you helped me. I'll be in touch. Make sure you don't get tweezered by that brat next door.

Love Jax Bord 3rd

Maybe Jax would come back one day. Sammy hoped so.

Chapter 5
More of Ellie

When Luke got home he went straight to the bathroom and locked himself in.

"Ellie?" he called. "Are you there?"

Then he waited. For a while he couldn't see or hear anything. At last a faint shape began to appear. It was Ellie, or at least it was some of Ellie. All Luke could see was one half of her body, and half her head. And she was standing in the toilet bowl.

Our books are tested
for children and young people by
children and young people.

Thanks to everyone who consulted on
a manuscript for their time and effort in
helping us to make our books better
for our readers.

More from *Barrington Stoke*...

Space Ace
ERIC BROWN

Billy dreams of flying in space, so he can't wait to take a trip around the Earth with his grandad.

But then the ship's computer takes over and they zoom off on a tour of the solar system!

Will they ever make it home?

The Story of Matthew Buzzington
ANDY STANTON

Matthew Buzzington can turn into a fly. Imagine that!

It's just that, well, he hasn't yet.

But with robbers and flying pineapples out to get him he needs to make his super-power work!

Can he do it?

Mad Iris
JEREMY STRONG

Mad Iris doesn't like the ostrich farm. She likes Pudding Lane School much better!

But the men from the ostrich farm are hot on her trail...

Ross and Katie to the rescue!

Meet the Weirds
KAYE UMANSKY

Mrs Weird is a stunt woman. Mr Weird is a scientist with a habit of blowing up houses. Then there are the children and their black cat, Ginger.

Now the Weirds have moved in next door to the neatest, tidiest family ever.

Looks like things may get a little – well, weird!

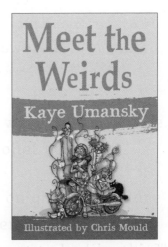

she said. "Well, I don't. I didn't want to drown and I never wanted to be a ghost. It's not much fun."

Luke was shocked. He thought it would be ace to be a ghost. You would be able to slide through walls and appear in places whenever you wanted. You could scare people. Cool! But then he remembered that he had something to tell Ellie. "I've discovered more about Charlie," he said. "He didn't drown."

Ellie's hand flew to her mouth. "He didn't?" she asked. "Do you know what happened to him?"

"Two years after you drowned there was a war," Luke said. "Charlie was killed in the war, after fighting in France."

"Oh, poor Charlie," Ellie said sadly. "Poor Charlie."

"Yuck! Do you have to stand there?" asked Luke.

"Yes, because I have to be in contact with water, remember?" said Ellie.

"But I can only see half of you," Luke complained.

"I need lots of water to make a full appearance," Ellie told him. "That's why I stood in the bath last time."

"You're weird," Luke said.

"I'm a ghost," Ellie answered. "I'm meant to be weird."

"Yes, but you're even weirder," said Luke. "Ghosts don't appear in toilet bowls."

"Oh, you're an expert on ghosts now, are you?" Ellie asked. Then her lip started to wobble. "Do you think I want to be like this?"

she said. "Well, I don't. I didn't want to drown and I never wanted to be a ghost. It's not much fun."

Luke was shocked. He thought it would be ace to be a ghost. You would be able to slide through walls and appear in places whenever you wanted. You could scare people. Cool. But then he remembered that he had something to tell Ellie. "I've discovered more about Charlie," he said. "He didn't drown."

Ellie's hand flew to her mouth. "He didn't?" she asked. "Do you know what happened to him?"

"Two years after you drowned there was a war," Luke said. "Charlie was killed in the war, after fighting in France."

"Oh, poor Charlie," Ellie said softly. "Poor Charlie."